# The
# Lonely Polar Bear

KHOA LE

Happy Fox
BOOKS

There was a snowstorm that
lasted for many days. The strong
wind was wailing and crying.

When the storm was finally over,
a polar bear slowly crawled
out of an icy cave.

He was quite small.

The little polar bear wandered
around the vast, snow-covered land,
looking for his mommy and his brothers.
Suddenly, he saw a strange thing—a
little spirit girl from the night sky.

"Bear!"

"Little friend!"

The little spirit girl climbed onto
the polar bear's back, and
they walked on and on.

They traveled very far . . .

. . . a long, long way together.

One night . . .

. . . They saw an amazing sight.

The little spirit girl said,
"Look, Bear, the northern lights!
My family is coming."

"It's time to come home!"

And so the polar bear kept
walking on his own.

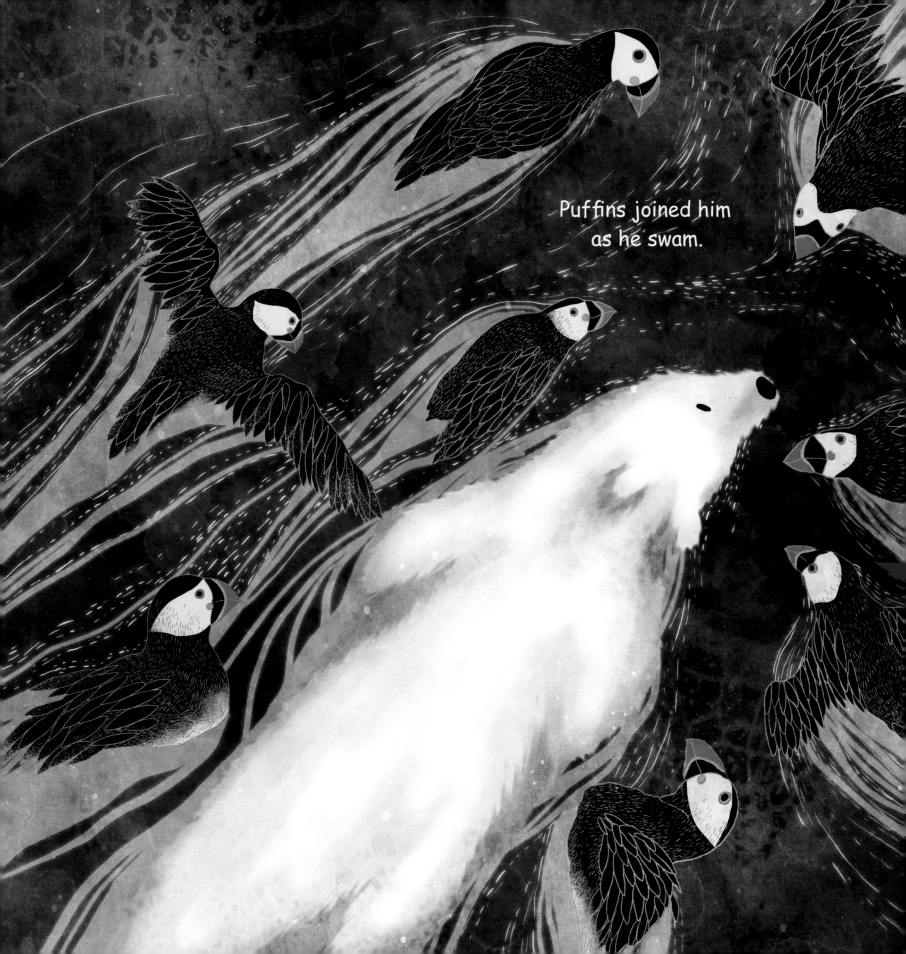

Puffins joined him
as he swam.

The polar bear
continued swimming.

The fish quickly
swam past him.

"Goodbye, bear!"

When the polar bear reached land,
he continued walking.

The elks greeted him with
a big "Helloooo!"

"Hello!" said the polar bear.
But he still hadn't found his family.

The polar bear made many
friends on his journey.

He met some noisy friends . . .

. . . and some quiet friends.

Time passed and the polar bear grew older.
Spring, summer, autumn, winter . . .

But he wasn't as big as he should have been.
There was little for him to eat
on the slowly melting ice.

Without his spirit friend,
he felt lost.

The polar bear fell asleep
and began to dream.

He saw the dark winter sky,
filled with glowing sparkles.

"Lonely bear, I have always kept an eye on you.
You can only see our light in winter, when
the sky is dark, but I am always here."

"It's okay, spirit friend, don't worry.
I made many other friends.
I'm not lonely anymore!"

Somewhere in the snowy North Pole,
a polar bear is sitting quietly and peacefully,
enjoying his beautiful sky filled with northern lights.

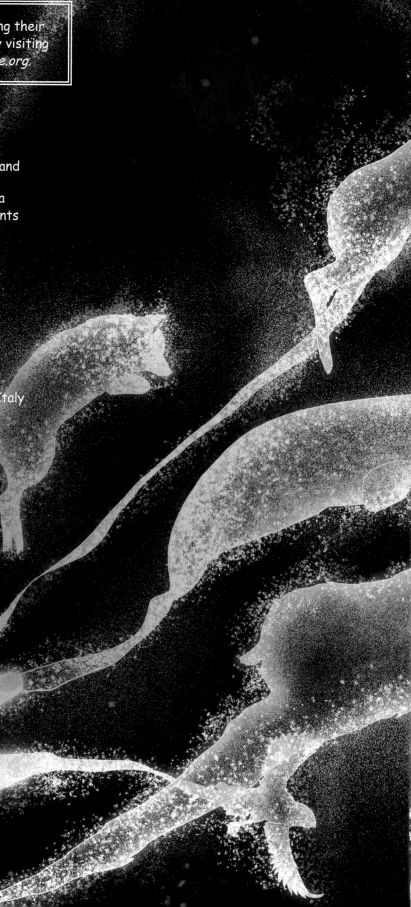

Polar bears face an uncertain future due to climate change that is causing their ice habitat to melt. Find out how you can help them survive and thrive by visiting online resources such as *polarbearsinternational.org* or *www.worldwildlife.org*.

Happy Fox Books is an imprint of Fox Chapel Publishing Company, Inc., 903 Square Street, Mount Joy, PA 17552.

© 2018 Snake SA, Chemin du Tsan du Péri 10, 3971 Chermignon, Switzerland

ISBN 978-1-64124-100-7 (paperback)
ISNB 978-1-64124-016-1 (hardcover)

Library of Congress Cataloging-in-Publication Data

Names: Lãe, Khoa (Artist), author, illustrator.
Title: The lonely polar bear / Khoa Lãe.
Other titles: Polare l'orso solitario. English
Description: Mount Joy : Happy Fox Books, 2018. | Originally published: Italy
    : Nuinui, 2016 under the title, Polare l'orso solitario. | Summary: An
    orphaned polar bear, accompanied for a while by a little girl, travels
    through the Arctic, seeking another of his kind. Includes information
    about polar bears and their habitat.
Identifiers: LCCN 2018012855 | ISBN 9781641240161 (hardcover)
Subjects: | CYAC: Polar bear—Fiction. | Bears—Fiction. | Orphaned
    animals—Fiction. | Arctic regions—Fiction.
Classification: LCC PZ7.1.L3897 Lon 2018 | DDC [E]—dc23
LC record available at https://lccn.loc.gov/2018012855

To learn more about the other great books from Fox Chapel Publishing, or to find a retailer near you, call toll-free 800-457-9112 or visit us at *www.FoxChapelPublishing.com*.

We are always looking for talented authors. To submit an idea, please send a brief inquiry to acquisitions@foxchapelpublishing.com.

Fox Chapel Publishing makes every effort to use environmentally friendly paper for printing.

Printed in Malaysia
Second printing

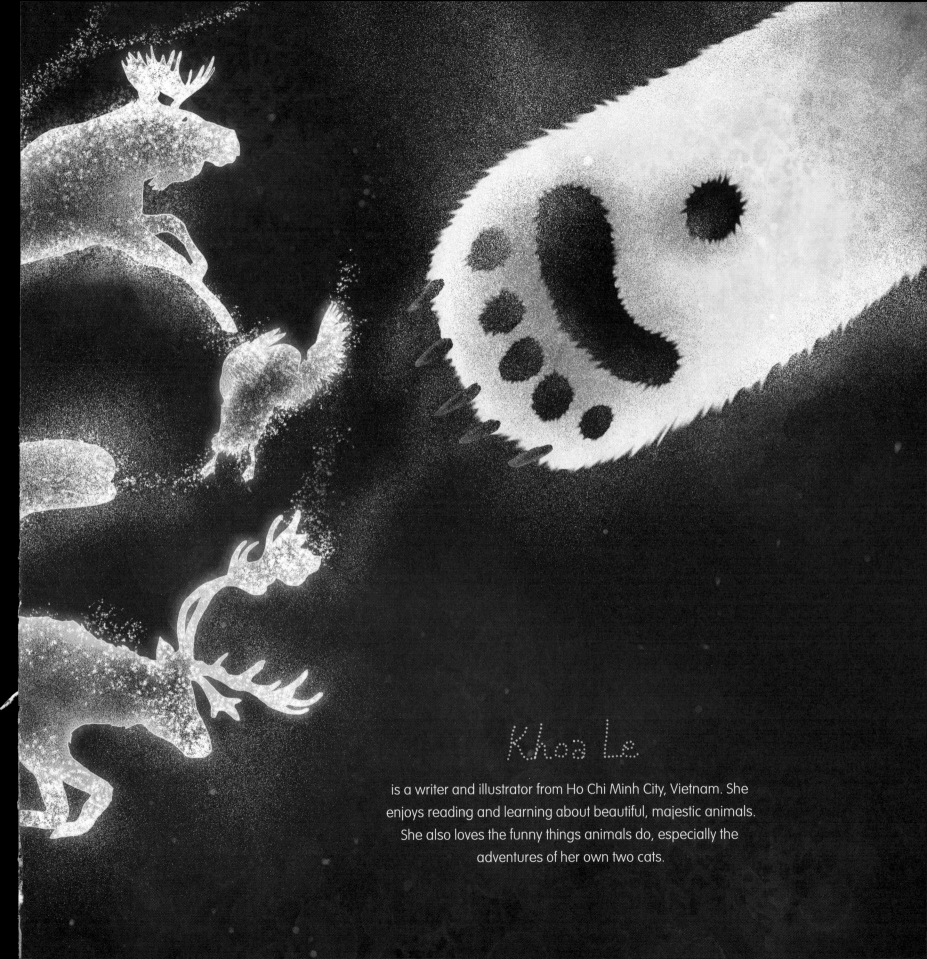

**Khoa Le**

is a writer and illustrator from Ho Chi Minh City, Vietnam. She enjoys reading and learning about beautiful, majestic animals. She also loves the funny things animals do, especially the adventures of her own two cats.